I0591337

The Moldy Orange Bandage

Book One

The Moldy Orange Bandage

Playbooks and Short Stories

Lirio Blanco Show

MOUNTAIN ARBOR
PRESS
Alpharetta, GA

Copyright © 2021 by Albalis D. Smith

All rights reserved. No part of this book may be reproduced or transmitted in any form or by any means, electronic or mechanical, including photocopying, recording, or any information storage and retrieval system, without permission in writing from the author.

ISBN: 978-1-6653-0129-9 - Paperback
eISBN: 978-1-6653-0130-5 - eBook

These ISBNs are the property of Mountain Arbor Press for the express purpose of sales and distribution of this title. The content of this book is the property of the copyright holder only. Mountain Arbor Press does not hold any ownership of the content of this book and is not liable in any way for the materials contained within. The views and opinions expressed in this book are the property of the Author/Copyright holder, and do not necessarily reflect those of Mountain Arbor Press.

Library of Congress Control Number: 2021918956

Printed in the United States of America   0 9 1 5 2 1

⊛ This paper meets the requirements of ANSI/NISO Z39.48-1992 (Permanence of Paper)

Cover Art: Professor Mark S. Smith with Steph Smith

Martha Argueta De Vargas
July 8, 1931-November 23, 2014

This book is dedicated to the memory of my mother, Martha Argueta De Vargas, who was an art lover and writer. I also wish to keep alive my connection with the arts. Without my mother's support and inspiration, the arts might have never become part of my life as they are today. Thanks "Mama!"

And also I dedicate this book to my daughter Steph. I want this book to become a concrete reminder for my daughter about the deep connection that she and my mother shared in this earthly realm. The innocent and unconditional love has bonded both together until this very day. My mom might have passed to a better life, but the memories of her love and sacrifice will be encrypted in my daughter's mind and soul forever.

"It's something that took me a long time to learn. I didn't start making any progress in my work until I gave up the idea of trying to [satisfy others] and started doing work for myself, because that's when you start writing from the heart, and then people will get it, strangely enough, and they will respond to it much more strongly."

— Matt Groening
Series Creator, *The Simpsons*

"As an actor, I want to thank all the casting directors and producers who rejected me horribly and never hired me and didn't like the way I looked and thought I was nerdy. Because without them like beating me down into the ground and making me depressed, I would never have picked up a pen and written my own thing, and did it myself, around the system. So I feel like this is what this night is about . . . to celebrate people not waiting for permission to make their art. You know I'm a—I'm a square peg and I've been trying to fit in the round Hollywood hole for a long time . . . So anyway, I hope that that inspires other people to do that . . . So thank you, thank you."

— Felicia Day (*The Guild*)
Won Best Female Actor in a Comedy Web Series, 2009

Table of Contents

Acknowledgments   *xi*

Introduction   *xv*

Preface   *xvii*

Section 1: Short Stories   1

Sigmund the Squirrel   3

Terry The Chipmunk   5

The Muddy Hole   8

Section 2: Theatrical Plays   15

Moldy Oranges   17

The Box of Bandages   51

Acknowledgments

Thanks to my mother, Martha Argueta De Vargas, who, besides being a professional nurse, was a passionate lover of the arts, theatrical director, and writer of newspaper articles and poetry. Because of this, I lived all my life surrounded by the arts in all its manifestations. I still remember her writings and poems which I recited in a considerable number of school arts festivals and competitions. In my memory, and thanks to her powerful influence, still encrypted are:

- Her newspaper articles in the newspaper "La Estrella De Panama"
- Memories of the ballet dancers of the "Compania Nacional De Danza De Panama"
- The paintings of great Panamanian masters, whose exhibitions were taken to my little native town David, Province of Chiriqui in the Republic of Panama, through the INAC and "La Casa De Bellas Artes De David," in which my mother was a very active member
- The presentations of the theatrical groups of the "Instituto David" and the "Marist School" (San Vicente De Paul School), where my mother was director and I was an actress
- The concerts of the "Orquestra Cuerdas De Chiriqui," currently known as the "Fundacion Mario De Obaldia Alvarado" and the Orquestra Sinfonica Juvenil, where I was a violoncello player

- The "Coro Sinfonico Nacional de Costa Rica" and "Frazer Memorial United Methodist Church in Montgomery, Alabama," where we both sang together
- The theatrical group "Renacer" from the "Universidad de Costa Rica," where she was director and I was her assistant director. In this group, I met a couple of the best women I have ever known
- The theatrical group of "Colegio El Rosario" in Costa Rica, where I had the great opportunity to be a director
- The theatrical groups from AUM (Auburn University at Montgomery, Alabama) and "The Lionheart theatre" in Norcross, Georgia, where I was set painter and designer
- For a while, and thanks to her support, I made my living painting murals and midsize paintings

Before she died, my mother supported and believed with all her heart in my husband's hard work involving puppets and live-action performances. She also helped him design and sew some of the outfits for Mark's puppets.

I also want to thank my father-in-law, Billy Ray Smith, and step mother-in-law, Katherine Greene Smith, for being loving grandparents, and my father, Guillermo Vargas Campos, for being a good father to me. I hope both men are in the presence of God, in the Heavenly realm.

Also, I want to thank my husband, Mark S. Smith, for being a loving father, husband, and son-in-law to my mother. Mark has helped me by editing the sloppy drafts I created, so that you, the audience, can understand my English, my second language. Also, I want to acknowledge him as the co-creator of the title of this book. Originally, I wanted to call it *Oranges and Bandages*, and he suggested calling it *The Moldy Orange Bandage*, which our editor and myself agree is a very original title for this book.

And finally, I want to thank God, for allowing me to have such a good daughter. Steph is a very good girl, but more than anything, she has a very big heart. Thanks to the wise advice my child has given me at times, I have based decisions on such insightful guidance, which later proved to be spot-on. I pray that God will watch out for her when I am no longer in the earthly realm.

Introduction

After finishing a painting, I want to have paint stains on my fingers. I like to see the remains of clay under my nails after completing a sculpture of a 3D character, or while I work in an architectural model of my own design. While painting a theatrical set, I feel proud when I wear paint-stained clothing.

After completing a piece of artwork, pottery, or craft of any sort, how many paint-stains or clay residue do electronic gadgets such as cell phones, tablets, and laptops leave under your nails? How many paint-stains? I believe we all know the answer to those questions.

God gave us hands to use them, and not to be replaced by the intangible force that runs through fiber-optic cables, radio waves, or any other signal that flies through the air. What will humankind do with all those technological gadgets and apps during an electrical power blackout? Are they going to feed, clothe, or protect us? I'll leave you to answer those questions by yourself.

In the meantime, I wish you to enjoy my little compilation of short stories and theatrical plays, which were created using strokes of pens, pencils, diverse color highlighters, crayons, and all on hardcover notebooks. Inevitably, I used technology to make my stories accessible for you, the audience. However, my thoughts would never have flown if it wasn't for the tangible handmade manuscript.

I hope you enjoy this journey from short stories to theatrical plays. I want to thank you all in advance for taking time to read this book. So, as others would say, grab your steaming cup of coffee, your pastry, your taco, or any other delicious appetizer and enjoy *The Moldy Orange Bandage*.

Very humbly,
Lirio Blanco Show

Preface

I have always been a creative person. In order to be fully creative, one has to develop the ability to transform concrete results from abstract ideas. When I was a young teenager, my mom was in charge of putting together a communication board; she used a white, bare poster board, trimmed it in the shape of a tree, and transformed it into the centerpiece. The concept of transcending from the concrete idea of a tree to a representation of a tree on a white poster board has stuck in my mind to this day.

For some time, I used to write little existentialist poems. Actually, more than anything else, they were endless fragments of thoughts; they were my desperate attempt to communicate my own consciousness.

As many of you know, becoming unemployed gives one the opportunity of brainstorming ideas for earning extra income during times of uncertainty. Every time I lost a job, art has been my most reliable way to get extra income. For that reason, between 2012 and 2013, I started writing children's short stories; eventually, I transitioned to stories geared to an older crowd. However, I was not able to go beyond a couple of paragraphs. While sitting and staring at the computer monitor, my stories could not unravel.

Seven years have passed since then. If it was not for the Covid-19 pandemic, I might have never considered writing anything again. The uncertainty that the virus has brought to humanity, in my particular case, worked as a creative catalyst. I dusted off a couple of drafts and made the decision to finish them; this time, I turned them into theatrical plays. To my surprise, this transition of format empowered me to finish them. No matter how unpolished one's creations might be, one should never toss an idea. When one is least expecting, inspiration can turn an idea into something very different than when it was conceived.

There is nothing more damaging for an artist than keeping backburner projects. Those sketches, recordings, or pieces of paper, which contain unfinished poems and articles, can become one's worst obstacle that can last a lifetime, if one is not careful.

The three short stories that started it all are presented in this book as a preamble to two theatrical plays. So that the readers can experience the transition between the two formats of writing, I would like to immerse them in the original short stories first.

Initially, this book was to contain three plays. Two target the family audience, the other adult. But after discussing the content with my editor, I decided to set aside the one targeting the adult audience for future editions.

THE THREE SHORT STORIES

As an animal lover, it comes as no surprise that my subconscious pulled animals to portray the characters of my short stories. While "The Muddy Hole" is based on my beloved dog Guzy and her impact in my life, "Sigmund The Squirrel" and "Terry the Chipmunk" are entirely fictional in nature.

About "Sigmund The Squirrel"

This is a story about self-identity preservation, government control of the masses, and compassion, which at the end, plays like the ultimate trait that connects humanity with nature.

About "Terry The Chipmunk"

"Terry the Chipmunk" portrays how appearances make humans more vulnerable creatures. We all share a common fear for self-preservation which makes us greedy. However, if we all don't learn to share, as we share the unique planet earth, where we all live, humans might end up hurt and alone.

About "The Muddy Hole"

Little did I know that a stray dog camping out in my front yard would become one of my most beloved lifetime companions. Although the two following short stories are fictional, this first one is a summary of the events surrounding how Guzy made the move into our house and our lives.

THE TWO THEATRICAL PLAYS

About Moldy Oranges

Moldy Oranges is a play partially based on actual family experiences. While my husband is American, I am Panamanian; therefore, there is a rich repertoire of circumstances that can be adapted to a theatrical play. When two individuals from different cultures get involved romantically and live under the same roof, many misunderstandings, conflicts, and awkward situations can arise. This only escalates further when an in-law is added to the equation. As many Latin Americans can relate, my mother lived with me, my daughter, and my husband during the last years of her life.

Having one's parent living in the same dwelling can be especially cumbersome. However, after losing my mother in 2014, I can say that I don't regret having her with me during those years. Yes, many times were extremely difficult, but there is no price for the love, compassion, faithfulness, tenderness, and care that my mother gave my daughter while she was alive.

About The Box of Bandages

The Box of Bandages is a play which targets the tween audience. It was originally written for my daughter Steph amidst the lockdown of the Covid-19 pandemic in 2020. Without getting into too much detail, The Box of Bandages is also partially based on the real events of January 2014, when there was a winter storm that paralyzed Atlanta for nearly a week. I wanted to use that experience as the setting of my play.

SECTION 1

Short Stories

Sigmund
the Squirrel

Sigmund Squirrel was a jumpy little fellow. He was cinnamon with little chips of creamy white covering his body. He would dance in circles, enjoying his beautiful forest.

But one day, fliers were spread all over Raccoon Hollow Town, inviting the residents to a town council meeting.

All animals attended, including Rickey the Badger, Lazy Possum, and Gladys the Rat. At the elongated table sat eight very important representatives of the community, headed by Theodore Fox Shame. He explained the convenience of having men build a new human complex that would require the destruction of Raccoon Hollow and also used rhetorical phrases implying the sacrifice of the community, which would inevitably benefit their children's future.

Sigmund stood up and fiercely opposed the idea. The Badger, the Raccoon, the Possum, and the Rat also stood up, yelling "No destruction! Long live Raccoon Hollow!"

But the narcissistic nature of the Fox would not be denied; his charismatic presence overwhelmed the voices of resistance, and soon the whole town voted yes to the action . . . opposed only by the five downhearted friends.

Everybody packed their humble belongings, and one by one, every family of rabbits, chipmunks, raccoons, and other various critters left the town's beautifully flowing streams, flowery meadows, and trees hanging with Spanish moss.

What a desolate scene it was soon to be.

The day of the demolition, the bulldozers and cranes were all set, when all of a sudden, the Squirrel and the Badger appeared screeching angrily, while the Possum and Rat stood in front of the bulldozers, confronting the men.

But the men were not to be stopped as they moved forward with their machinery, until they halted just inches from the brave critters.

The men were puzzled by the distinctive dignity of the animals, so they decided to adopt the creatures and allowed them to dwell freely in the open park at the center of the facility, with a pond in which the creatures could swim and play—the one area of tiny forest that was preserved of Raccoon Hollow. It now belonged to the brave animals who had remained behind to protect their home.

Terry
the Chipmunk

Terry the Chipmunk was running through the meadow when he caught a glance of beautiful acorns in the distance. He was hypnotized by their beauty. The acorns were fat and shiny. They captivated Terry's eyes. He did not waste time to run and start filling his cheeks with these attractive acorns.

His two cheeks were so puffy, and they got puffier, puffier, and puffier, until they both looked like a pair of furry water balloons.

However, Terry wanted these acorns all for himself . . . So he started to plan how to conceal them inside his cave. Realizing his neighbors would return soon, he became frantic, his eyes swelling with the emotion of owning these marvelous acorns.

Venus, one of his friends, approached him and he tried to run and hide from her. Curious, she chased him for some time until she cornered him against a tree root.

Terry was so afraid to share his nuts that he pressed his teeth together protectively to hide them . . . tighter, tighter, and tighter until—Snap! Crack! Ping!

Tiny pieces of his teeth began to chip off.

Hearing a desperate yelp from Terry, Venus tried to get a better look. Somehow, she convinced him to open his mouth. Not only did the shiny acorns fall to the cavern floor, but tiny pieces of pearly white incisors, the two front teeth Terry had been so proud of, tumbled all over the ground.

Terry kneeled down in disbelief and cried and cried and cried in his distress, sobbing "What a pain, oh, what a pain!"

Feeling compassion for her friend, despite his greedy behavior, Venus tried to calm Terry down. Terry couldn't stop crying until, suddenly, he realized among the spilled acorns, he saw all that was left of his beloved incisors. He held his head with his two paws in disbelief and scrambled to rapidly retrieve his treasures. This time Venus clutched a few in her own paws to challenge his attention.

She held one paw out, and Terry hesitated. Venus smiled at him warmly, and

when Terry saw her teeth reflecting the radiant sunlight, he remembered his own lost teeth. Terry dropped the few acorns in his grasp and his fingers touched his naked gums with the realization that he had lost something far more precious than a few acorns . . .

He had lost his teeth.

Venus explained that, had he not been so greedy by trying to hide the extra acorns—more than he could have ever eaten all winter—he would never have broken his teeth.

"But don't worry, Terry," she continued soothingly, patting his quivering paw with her own, "Dr. Drill, the Chipmunk dentist, will fix your teeth."

Terry replied, now calm, "Thanks Venus . . . but will you take me to him?"

"Of course," Venus said. "But next time, Terry, you have to remember—when we give to someone, we are entitled to receive as well."

THE END!

The Muddy Hole

One rainy afternoon, a soaking wet ball of fur was lying in a muddy hole . . . "That thing" dug in front of the house where I lived at that time. It was twisted like a pretzel, trying to protect itself from the rain. I discovered its presence in our front yard and could not feel more repulsion; I thought, *This awful animal must be a nest of fleas and other pests; I should get rid of it right now.* Without thinking, I threw little pebbles to this awful presence, and it growled at me. I could not feel more furious than a Tasmanian she-devil with bloated eyes while experiencing a tantrum full of rage. Then I threw a bucket of water at it, and finally, it left.

The next day, again, it was in the muddy hole. I threw bigger pebbles this time and yelled at it, "Go away, you awful invader!" and it growled at me again.

In those days, I was still mourning the death of my father, who died recently. His passing changed the course of my own life, with the realization that without him, my family's core vanished partially. But life went on.

Day by day, I started looking at the furry animal with fresh eyes; I decided to throw cheesy puffs to it, and the beast seemingly sneered at them. What a snobby animal! I thought.

One day, it was not in the hole, and another day passed and it was not there. Surprisingly, I found myself quite disappointed and started looking for it around the neighborhood; I found it at the rear of a neighbor's garage. I called it, and it ignored me. I threw meat at it and did not get any response. I became very sad.

I lost it, I thought.

In a few days, it returned to the hole; I could not be happier. But other neighbors wanted it as well. Some brought it meat cutlets; others came, telling me they wanted it for their own pet. Then, my sister Mary suggested bringing her inside the house. I became very happy. I bought her a doggie bowl, food, collar, a leash, and a medicated flea collar.

Finally, I got inside the secluded front yard, where the muddy hole was located, took her in my arms like a baby, and she actually let me take her inside the house. Needless to say, she adapted to the surroundings very quickly.

She was bathed, brushed, and I kissed her many times with so much love and tenderness. I named her Augusta Vargas, after the name of a fictional writer I saw on TV, with the nickname "Guzy." She became the most important and most beautiful treasure I ever had at that stage of my life. But she got the idea she could do whatever pleased her, like lying on the beds and couches and grabbing human food from the top of the dining table.

Evidently, Guzy was potty trained. But we did not count that she was a girl capable of attracting the most persistent suitors from the entire neighborhood. The parade of admirers was very entertaining; one we called "Lion," another "Little Piece of Poo," "Mangy," "Blacky," and the others just came by their own accord.

Nevertheless, after doubting any procreative capabilities of our new pet, a Jehovah's Witness, who used to visit us regularly, announced to us, "This little girl is expecting a litter." We did not believe that this newcomer, whom we literally had forced into a diaper (complete with a bow on her head), was carrying new life in her tummy. All doubts disappeared on that fateful day, when she delivered a beautiful black puppy. Seemingly, Guzy had chosen "Blacky," the most persistent of all, as the proud father of her puppy.

Not long afterward, we moved to another country and she traveled inside a crate in the airplane's cargo hold. I panicked the whole flight, until I saw her crate lying on the claim section at the airport. Her eyes were bulged out due to her own panic from the sound of the plane's engine.

When time passed, I realized that the perception of living in another environment differs between animals and humans. While animals adapt easily, humans take more time.

For circumstances beyond my control, Guzy had to remain in a stranger's house, where she was mistreated while we lived in a little apartment. During that period of time, she lost lots of weight and hair and missed us so much. Then, I was determined to fight and fight to have her back in our arms, until she finally returned. Our darling Guzy regained her appetite (and naturally the weight along with it), regrew her hair, and renewed her cheerful outlook . . . and energy!

She was capable of jumping on top of tables, and grabbed a wrapped rotisserie chicken, opened it, and ate it completely. She loved glazed cinnamon rolls, and her ability to sneak in silence was remarkable. As she was a sheepdog, Guzy pushed our legs with the top of her head; and it was not until a new puppy named Gioconda (Yoki) arrived, when Guzy started to show us, late in life, her full repertoire of affection.

Later, her health declined in many different ways, making her my greatest endeavor. At that particular time, I made it my priority to fight her illnesses no matter what, and thus prolong her life. She was a survivor, "a trooper" as many Doctors referred to her. There was a time when she ran away and ended up near a very busy highway. She did not hesitate to cross it right at the traffic light; there, a vet technician was waiting for the light to change from red to green. When she saw Guzy about to cross, the technician got out of her car, pulling the dog inside. Obviously, I was not aware of all these events due to my deep sorrow for losing her, when all of a sudden, the vet technician called us and said she was holding Guzy at her clinic, ready to be picked up. It was a truly beautiful miracle!

As so many dog lovers out there know, well, we finally lost her. It has been thirteen years since Guzy went to Doggie Heaven, and although I keep her ashes in my closet, my human brain has let go of many memories about her. But there is one memory I will never forget.

Distant in space and time, in that two-story house where I lived very briefly, was that muddy hole that gave Guzy protection and warmth. The same hole from which I wanted to evict her, unaware that the muddy hole, harbored for my mother and me, may be one of the most beautiful gifts of our lives. For all those who find their own uninvited guest in a muddy hole in their own front yards, I recommend you think twice before evicting it, because maybe, that dirty, musty, and muddy hole is the sweetest trap and will help to catch your hearts for an everlasting lifetime.

"In Memory of my beloved Guzy"
1991(?)-2007

SECTION 2

Theatrical Plays

The Moldy Oranges

CAST:

KIRA
REGINA
ALEXA
DONOFRIO
CARMEN
THE ORANGES PUPPETS

(The scene is a small kitchen, half lit. KIRA is singing, dancing, wearing kitchen gloves. She wipes the stove. While cleaning it, she shakes her hips, turns front, back, shakes right and left, and continues to sing. She wears a turquoise dress with an apron and big glasses. Her reddish hair is fastened back into a big bun. After cleaning the stove, she takes a pot, fills it with water, lights one of the burners, and sets the pot of water on top. Someone knocks on the back door. KIRA opens it and REGINA, the next-door neighbor, makes her entry.)

REGINA:
Good morning, Kira. How are you today?

KIRA:
Come on inside, Regina, sit please.

(KIRA motions to a chair, and REGINA sits, making herself comfortable.)

REGINA:
Thanks, sweetie.

KIRA:
Would you like me to put the kettle on? I saw one at the mall, baby, and I had to get it, I had to get it . . .

REGINA:
Modernizing the kitchen, huh?

KIRA:
Oh, you know, change is always good, I tell you that.

(She points to the choices of teas.)

KIRA:
Which tea would you like, Regina?

REGINA:
No coffee? What is all this about teas? Are you becoming irregular?

KIRA:
Oh no, no, no . . . I just want to acquire some refinement from my long-gone British ancestry. You know we have to always keep our ties to our ancestry.

REGINA:
(Aside) In her case, she probably got it from a crop-duster plane . . . as a little mist.

KIRA:
What did you say, sweetie?

REGINA:
Oh, no, nothing . . . That being in your house makes me feel so much joy . . . as if I'm in an airplane!
(While the two women are chatting, the stove catches on fire. KIRA jumps up and gestures wildly.)

KIRA:
Lordy mercy, my stove's on fire!

REGINA:
Oh my word!

(The two scramble to put out the fire, KIRA growing more and more hysterical, and REGINA attempting to calm her down. KIRA begins to hyperventilate as REGINA puts out the fire.)

REGINA:

Now don't worry, sweetie! We'll put it out! Just calm down. Land sakes!

KIRA:

(Gasping) Now you see what I mean? These are the things I have to deal with . . .

REGINA:

What do you mean?

KIRA:

That's got to be the handiwork of my son-in-law.

REGINA:

But Kira, I was sitting right here when the fire started. And he couldn't possibly have anything to do with it.

KIRA:

Ha ha ha ha! You see? That's exactly what he wants us all to believe. I know that rascal like the palm of my hand . . .

REGINA:

What do you mean?

KIRA:

He probably made some faulty . . . wiring . . . arrangement thing in the stove so that the fire started! Trying to make it look like it was my fault . . . just like him!

REGINA:

Sweetie, the pot of water flew over and made the burner's flames reach the clock. Don't you remember?

KIRA:

That's exactly what he wants all of us to believe.

(KIRA begins pacing back and forth, wandering aimlessly as though trying to find something, muttering gibberish.)

REGINA:
Calm, calm, Kira . . . Everything is going to be all right.

(ALEXA, KIRA's daughter, enters with a bag of groceries.)

ALEXA:
Regina! How are you?

(The two women hug.)

REGINA:
Fine, fine, and you?

ALEXA:
I am great, but what happened here? Mom! Are you okay? (Gasps) Oh my word, the stove!

KIRA:
(Crying hysterically) No! No, that was not my fault! That is the handiwork of your useless husband! I will not be blamed for that!

ALEXA:
What? What do you mean?

REGINA:
Alexa, the stove caught on fire for a moment, and we put it out. That's all. Nobody got hurt.

KIRA:
Oh, it caught on fire, all right! And it was your husband . . . He made this happen!

ALEXA:
Oh? And how did he manage that?

KIRA:
He probably arranged the stove . . . circuit . . . fire thingy to burn. Just so you would then blame ME! Blame your own mother! (Cries loudly)

ALEXA:
So, isn't he at the house right now?

REGINA:
No, Alexa, I haven't the faintest idea where he's at.

ALEXA:
Oh, Donofrio, where are you?

KIRA:
That Donofrio is not even good enough to hammer a little tiny nail in this house . . .

ALEXA:
Ugh! Are you going to start? Honestly! I barely crossed the threshold of this house, and already you have started . . .

(REGINA quietly gets up from the chair, looking uncomfortable.)

REGINA:
I better leave, Alexa.

ALEXA:
I am so sorry that you have had to witness this very strange incident.

REGINA:
It's just fine, girl. I will talk to you later, after . . . uh, yeah, just after.

(ALEXA walks REGINA to the door. KIRA sits down calmly and serves herself a cup of tea, then starts humming a song. ALEXA checks out the damage to the stove. While ALEXA approaches KIRA, the latter's demeanor changes. ALEXA notices, circling around, and goes back to begin unpacking the groceries and sorting them.)

KIRA:
I am curious to see what he did to the stove.

ALEXA:
Mom, I don't know. I really don't.

(ALEXA pulls a bag of oranges out of the groceries. KIRA stares at them, freezes in disbelief, and then immediately stands up.)

KIRA:
You got oranges? You realize how expensive they are now?

ALEXA:
Yes, but Carmen likes them, Mom.

KIRA:
Oh, the girl likes the oranges! The girl! Why don't you admit for whom you buy those oranges? Huh? Hah?

ALEXA:
Mom! Calm down!

KIRA:
How can I calm myself down? Oranges are so expensive! With all the money you two dummies spend on oranges, you could save for the child's braces.

ALEXA:
Mom, you are embarrassing me . . . Don't you see?

KIRA:
Oh-ho! Embarrassing you? I am just being realis-
tic . . . Your supposed husband is like a child (mock-
ing childish voice) "Oh, I am a little baby . . . who
needs to drink my baby bottle."

(KIRA sticks her thumb in her mouth, sucks it a few
times, and begins crying like a baby.)

(CARMEN, ALEXAS's daughter, enters.)

CARMEN:
Hello!

KIRA:
Oh, my adorable little baby!

(KIRA rushes over and pushes CARMEN's head toward her chest.)

CARMEN:
(Muffled) What happened, Nanita?

KIRA:
Oh, my child, my child! I cannot describe my sorrow.
See! My own daughter . . . is buying oranges for
your daddy. Little baby daddy depriving you from
that so well-needed . . . well-deserved Vitamin C . . .

(KIRA begins weeping deeply.)

CARMEN:
Grandma, I don't even like oranges!

ALEXA:
You see, Mom? She doesn't even like oranges, so please!
Please stop this mutiny! Please?

(KIRA pushes CARMEN away from her chest.)

KIRA:
How dare you say that? I have given my life for
you . . . You know what? I am so out of here . . . Ay,
yi-yi...

(KIRA storms out, crying and shaking her arms to the
ceiling)

CARMEN:
What was all that about, Mom?

ALEXA:
I think your abuela is going crazy.

(CARMEN pulls out a juice box from the grocery bag
and sips it casually.)

CARMEN:
Hm. You think?

(KIRA bursts back into the room, with a bag of green,
moldy rotten oranges. She pulls out one and shoves it
in ALEXA's face.)

KIRA:
You see this? I found these in the pantry . . . They are
green as money, and you wasted both oranges AND
money. There! See the connection? Huh? Ha!

(The lights dim, and three orange puppets come out.)

PUPPET ORANGES:
Green . . . Mad . . . Money . . .
Green . . . Mold . . . Money . . .
Green . . . Moldy . . . Money . . .
Juicy sweetness gone!
Juicy sweetness gone . . .

(The lights dim again.)

KIRA, ALEXA AND CARMEN (together):
What was that?

(The girls surround where the oranges are lying. The three look directly to the oranges.)

(The puppet oranges are pulled offstage by a string.)

(ALEXA and KIRA follow them and exit, while CARMEN performs a solo with her ukulele.)

CARMEN:
What was that about?

(DONOFRIO enters.)

ALEXA:
Where have you been?

DONOFRIO:
Oh, I was just getting some oranges!

ALEXA:
(Growls) Why? Mom already had a fit about the moldy ones in the pantry!

DONOFRIO:
Why not? I work hard.

KIRA:
Hardly, you mean . . .

DONOFRIO:
Senora!

KIRA:
No "senora" me! (Goes downstage) Humph!

(KIRA crosses her arms while DONOFRIO starts arranging the oranges in a bowl.)

(KIRA approaches the table where the bowl is and looks at the oranges with disdain. She scowls at DONOFRIO and leaves the scene.)

ALEXA:
Donofrio, what are we going to do about this situation? You know, Mom told me that you sabotaged the stove to catch on fire. Is that true? Why would you want to burn the stove, Donofrio?

(DONOFRIO starts laughing hard.)

DONOFRIO:
Why should I want to burn my own freaking stove? Just think about it, will you?

ALEXA:
(Hysterical) I don't know, maybe Mom is right. You just want to make her life more difficult.

DONOFRIO:
More difficult? More difficult? Do you think I want to create difficulty to make more difficult my already difficult life? Make more difficult, what is already . . . difficult?

ALEXA:
You tell me?

(CARMEN enters.)

CARMEN:
(Awkwardly) Am I interrupting anything?

ALEXA:
Of course not . . . (Suddenly) I got an idea!

DONOFRIO AND CARMEN (together):
What idea?

ALEXA:
When you buy your oranges, hide them in your closet
upstairs!

CARMEN:
Great idea! Grandma won't notice them, then.

DONOFRIO:
Do you think it will work?

ALEXA:
Yes! I know it will work.

(ALEXA, CARMEN and DONOFRIO shake each other's hands simultaneously, as though making a group
deal.)

(Lights dim down.)

INTERMISSION

(KIRA is seated, watching her soap opera. She is snapping green beans. CARMEN enters.)

CARMEN:
Can I help you, Nanita?

KIRA:
Of course, my little queen! Come on and sit next to me, then.

(She extends her arms toward the little girl and hugs her as she sits down, obviously enjoying the tender moment.)

CARMEN:
Why are you doing that to the green beans, Nanita?

KIRA:
The green beans have a little thread. If you leave them while cooking, when you eat them, you will feel them . . . and it is not pleasant.

CARMEN:
Ahh! Can I help?

KIRA:
Sure, my life!

(ALEXA enters.)

ALEXA:
It appears that the stove is looking good, Mom!

KIRA:
Ha ha . . . Let's see when the dummy is going to stage another disaster.

ALEXA:
Talking about red beans . . . Regina has asked me to guard an item for her here at our house.

KIRA:
What item? Why us?

ALEXA:
No one said "us," Mom. She asked me directly. Anyhow, I just want to let you know, I am going to help her.

KIRA:
Unh-unhhh . . . I wouldn't do it if I was you . . . But of course, I am nothing in this house. It is as if I am painted on the wall!

CARMEN:
Nanita, but we love you so much!

KIRA:
I know baby . . . Only you, only you!

ALEXA:
Ah Mom, you're always thinking the worst about people.

KIRA:
All these years have taught me that, Alexa!

(There is a knock at the door. ALEXA approaches the door and opens it to see REGINA.)

ALEXA:
Regina! Come on in!

REGINA:
Thanks, Alexa!

KIRA:
Regina, Regina . . . How nice to see you! It is always so
   good to have you here!

REGINA:
Carmen, how are you, sweetie?

CARMEN:
I am great!

(They hug briefly.)

ALEXA:
Regina, I already told Mom about the favor you need
   from us.

REGINA:
(Suspiciously) Uh . . . Okay?

CARMEN:
What . . . is it the item?

ALEXA:
Unh-unh . . . Carmen, go to your room. The adults are
   going to talk now.

CARMEN:
You always do that, Mom! You never spend time with
   me! Have you realized that?

ALEXA:
Carmen! What on earth are you talking about?

CARMEN:
Yes, Mom, you never play or talk to me when you are
   available.

KIRA:

Do you see what you have done? Come, my baby, come . . .

(CARMEN approaches KIRA and hugs her.)

KIRA:

You only live for "el sopenco" de Donofrio . . . El Don— NO! Grande! Uh!

ALEXA:

Mom, we have company here!

KIRA:

I don't care! Carmen, let's go, sweetie . . . Let's get out of here!

(KIRA and CARMEN exit.)

ALEXA:

Oh dear, Regina. I don't know what you think of us . . . Always fighting . . . always the drama!

REGINA:

Oh no, girl! All families fight like this.

ALEXA:

Did you bring what you wanted me to hold for you?

REGINA:

Sure, honey, I really appreciate this favor.

ALEXA:

Oh . . . It's nothing.

REGINA:

Are you sure?

ALEXA:
Sure. What are neighbors for?

(REGINA gets a box out of her big handbag and passes it to ALEXA.)

REGINA:
Here it is.

ALEXA:
I will go ahead and put it in the top of the closet, where no one can see it.

(DONOFRIO enters.)

DONOFRIO:
Hello!

REGINA:
Hello, neighbor! Well, I was just about to leave.

DONOFRIO:
You don't have to leave just because I came!

REGINA:
Oh no, Dono, I have to cook supper for the crowd at home.

ALEXA:
Thanks for stopping by, Regina.

(REGINA leaves.)

DONOFRIO:
Where are the other girls?

ALEXA:
I need you to put this box on the top shelf of our closet, would you?

DONOFRIO:
Yes, of course. But I asked where my daughter and your mom are.

ALEXA:
Ah, they are in Mom's bedroom . . . Carmen says I don't spend time with her and left crying.

DONOFRIO:
Well, only you would know, Alexa. You spend too much time at work and dealing with your mom's drama.

ALEXA:
Maybe you are right.

(KIRA makes her entry.)

DONOFRIO:
I am going to see my Carmen.

KIRA:
What did Regina ask you to hold for her? Ah?

ALEXA:
I don't know . . . And I don't WANT to know . . . Okay?

KIRA:
What if it's a bomb? Ah?

ALEXA:
Oh come on, Mom. Don't be an alarmist.

KIRA:
I would snoop . . . if I was you.

ALEXA:
Definitely not, Mom!

KIRA:
No? Not even the words of your own daughter help to
   make you react? Hah?

ALEXA:
What does that have to do with all this?

KIRA:
How am I going to sleep with that . . . that box here?

(KIRA walks side to side anxiously and then pauses
briefly.)

KIRA:
We should see what is inside.

ALEXA:
I forbid you, Mom!

KIRA:
Where is it?

ALEXA:
I won't tell you! And that is the last I will hear about
   this . . .

(ALEXA leaves, then KIRA starts pacing around
nervously.)

KIRA:
What would it be? Ay! I have to know! Humph . . . Who
   is going to stop me?

(KIRA looks around, making sure she isn't being watched, and exits the scene stealthily.)

(Lights go down.)

(A small light switches on in a simulated closet.)

KIRA:
Where could it be?

(KIRA searches among clothes, checks the bottom shelf and upper shelf. There she suddenly finds a bag wrapped in clothes.)

KIRA:
Ah-ha! I found it . . . I found it! Ha-ha-ha-ha-ha!

(KIRA takes the package down and sits in a chair with the bundle in her lap. She rapidly begins to unwrap it, takes the plastic bags out of the wrapping, and suddenly stops. KIRA looks petrified with her discovery. She looks to the audience, absolutely shocked.)

(The lights dim down, the closet is removed, and the lights go up again.)

(KIRA enters, still with a horrified look on her face.)

(ALEXA and CARMEN make their entry.)

CARMEN:
Nanita? What happened to you? Tell me . . .

ALEXA:
Mom! Please, tell me what happened? Please, Mom . . .

KIRA:
(Shocked) I cannot believe it, Alexa! I never believed
  someone could be capable of such a despicable act!

CARMEN:
Nanita, please? What is it?

ALEXA:
What is in that bag?

KIRA:
Something indescribable, Alexa . . . Something vile!
  Unbelievable!

ALEXA:
Show me, Mom! Is it Regina's bag? Did you find it?

(KIRA leaves the room in tears.)

ALEXA:
Mom, wait, please!

CARMEN:
Nanita, come back!

ALEXA:
Mom! Mom?

CARMEN:
What is going on, Mom?

ALEXA:
I don't know, baby, I don't know! I am afraid that
  Regina might have given us something to guard
  that was . . . inappropriate . . .

CARMEN:
Do you actually not know what it is?

ALEXA:
Not really . . . I didn't want to be rude, you know.

CARMEN:
But Mom, how could you agree to keep something unknown for someone? It could be dangerous . . . What are we going to do now?

ALEXA:
I don't know! I don't know . . . What should we do?

(DONOFRIO enters.)

DONOFRIO:
What is going on? Why these frightened faces?

CARMEN:
Dad, do you remember when Regina asked us to keep something for her, here at our home?

DONOFRIO:
Sure I do, I even placed it myself, on the top shelf of my closet.

ALEXA:
Did you . . . catch a glance of what it was?

DONOFRIO:
No! Certainly not . . . How could you think that about me?

ALEXA:
Don't you think it is risky to keep something unknown . . . from anyone?

DONOFRIO:
Sweetie, Regina is our long-time friend and neighbor. How could you think something bad about her?

ALEXA:
Look, Dono, my mother just left in tears, carrying a
    wrapped bag of something in her hands.

CARMEN:
Yes, Dad! She was crying very hard!

DONOFRIO:
I am speechless . . . Did your Mom snoop in my freak-
    ing closet? I cannot believe it . . . What disrespect
    from her! I never touch her belongings . . . I am go-
    ing to confront her right now!

ALEXA AND CARMEN (together):
No, no, don't . . .

DONOFRIO:
And why not? This is my house!

(KIRA enters with the wrapped bag.)

KIRA:
There is no need for you to look for me, "sopenco!"
    And yes, I was snooping in your closet . . . I have all
    the rights to protect this family!

ALEXA:
Protect this family? From what?

KIRA:
From the abuse! Yes, abuse!

CARMEN:
What is it in the bag, Nanita? Please, tell us?

(There is a knock on the door, and ALEXA walks over
to open it. REGINA is standing outside.)

REGINA:
Hi, Alexa, how are—

ALEXA:
Just what the heck did you give us to keep for you, Regina?

REGINA:
What are you talking about?

DONOFRIO:
Regina, please tell us . . . what is inside that bag?

CARMEN:
Yes, please!

REGINA:
Why should I tell you? It's something personal.

ALEXA:
That is not what my mother thinks about it, Regina. She says it is vile, unbelievable!

REGINA:
What? Vile? How come?

KIRA:
Did Regina have something to do with this bag? This is a conspiracy! I cannot believe it.

REGINA:
Of course I have something to do with the bag. I gave it to you guys! Don't you remember?

(KIRA begins wagging her finger at REGINA accusingly.)

THE MOLDY ORANGE BANDAGE

KIRA:
You? You? I can't believe it!

(REGINA backs away submissively, her hands up in surrender.)

ALEXA:
Enough! Mom, show us what is in the bag!

REGINA:
No . . . no . . . no . . . not my bag!

(REGINA walks toward KIRA to take the bag out of her hands, and the two begin a tug-of-war. During the tussle, the bag falls to the floor . . . and several oranges roll out.)

REGINA AND CARMEN:
(Disbelievingly) Oranges? Whose are those?

(KIRA swings her accusing finger out and around toward DONOFRIO.)

KIRA:
Yes, you! Why don't you tell all of us, whose oranges are those?

DONOFRIO:
Well . . .

(Everyone looks around at each other while awaiting his response.)

DONOFRIO (CONTD.):
Those oranges are ours!

KIRA:
Ha ha ha! Ours? Ours! Why don't you tell your wife, my own daughter, that you have been hiding these oranges in your closet? I dare you to deny it! Oh . . . poor baby! Needs oranges! How ridiculous!

REGINA:
So where is MY bag?

ALEXA:
Oh, shut up, Regina, and be quiet!

REGINA:
Oh, it's on now . . . How dare you, Alexa, speak to me like that? Are you crazy? Enough is enough. If you don't give me back my bag, I am going to sue you and your entire family . . .

(All four adults begin arguing incoherently with one another. CARMEN begins pacing around the room, watching with a suspicious look in her eyes. She kneels down and picks up the oranges, one by one, from the floor and carefully places them on top of the dining table. Calmly watching the argument as it escalates, she then glances at the audience and rolls her eyes, sighing heavily. She picks up a single orange and begins to peel it, then begins to eat it. After a few bites, CARMEN begins coughing hard, puts her hands on her chest, as her face begins to turn red. She motions to her throat, trying to signal the others that she's choking. Suddenly, CARMEN collapses on the floor and stops moving. ALEXA turns toward CARMEN with a shocked realization that her daughter is lying on the floor.)

ALEXA:
Carmen! (Shrieking) Carmen?

(A deep silence overtakes the room, the lights dim, and a spotlight on CARMEN starts to brighten.)

(ALEXA and KIRA kneel down next to CARMEN in complete silence.)

ALEXA:
Mom, is she okay?

KIRA:
Oh God, she is alive, but her pulse . . . it's so weak. She is purple. Oh God! What happened?

ALEXA:
(Crying) I don't know! Mom! What are we going to do? What are we going to do?

(REGINA pushes the two aside and kneels down over CARMEN.)

REGINA:
Get out of my way, you two!

DONOFRIO:
Yes, let Regina check Carmen! She's a nurse!

REGINA:
Her face is purple . . . blue . . . She must have eaten or swallowed something that has blocked her airway.

DONOFRIO:
But what?

(DONOFRIO begins walking, looking around, and notices the orange peels on the table.)

DONOFRIO:
She ate oranges! She ate oranges, but how could that cause her to choke?

REGINA:
The seeds! The seeds, Donofrio . . . Come on . . . Help me lift her. We need to proceed with the Heimlich maneuver!

(DONOFRIO lifts up CARMEN while REGINA supports her from behind and then presses her chest to forcefully eject the seed. REGINA makes several attempts to no avail while ALEXA and KIRA are desperately crying in the background.)

REGINA:
Oh no! Oh no, Carmen! This . . . is not your day, sweetie, no . . . Not today. C'mon, Donofrio, lay her on the floor again . . . Come on!

(DONOFRIO follows her directions, and REGINA starts thrusting her fists against CARMEN's chest, alternating with mouth-to-mouth resuscitation. After three attempts, CARMEN starts coughing and spits out the seeds. All surround her and give a collective sigh of relief.)

CARMEN:
(Still coughing) What happened?

REGINA:
If it wasn't for your little choking scene here, I was about to lay someone ELSE out in this room. Anybody want to guess who?

(REGINA stares down ALEXA, who backs away.)

REGINA (CONTD.):
Or why?

CARMEN:
(Coughing less) No! No idea . . .

REGINA:
Because your mother started talking to me the same way you talk to each other in this house—with disrespect to me and total disregard to my feelings. That is why . . . and that my girl, that is not going to happen . . . again!

ALEXA:
But Regina . . .

REGINA:
Oh no! No, Alexa . . . This time, you . . . and the rest of you . . .

(REGINA points accusingly at KIRA and DONOFRIO.)

REGINA (CONTD.):
. . . are going to be quiet . . . and listen to what I have to say. Get that child some water.

(DONOFRIO nods meekly and fetches a glass of water for CARMEN, who is still lying on the floor. He kneels down and gives it to her.)

REGINA:
Do you see this girl lying on the floor? She is the victim here! Yes . . . she is.

KIRA:
How dare you, Regina, talk to us like that?

REGINA:

My question to you, Kira . . . is how dare you talk to your family the way you do? You talk to neighbors . . . strangers on the street you never laid eyes on in your life . . . with more respect than you talk to your family. Why is that?

(KIRA tilts her head down meekly, in tears.)

REGINA (CONTD.):

I have been visiting this house for more than fifteen years, and I know more than anybody else the great love that bonds this family together. You all have been through hardships and joyful events, but always bickering about the most miniscule things . . . While doing so, today, all of you might have lost the most precious thing in all your lives . . . Carmen, this sweet girl . . . who never harms anybody, a creature full of love and innocence.

(REGINA pauses briefly, and silence envelopes the room.)

KIRA:

Alexa . . . Donofrio . . . please forgive me. Please, both of you . . .

(KIRA breaks down and cries.)

ALEXA:

Only if you forgive me, too!

(Both women hug warmly, then the two kneel and reunite with CARMEN on the floor.)

REGINA:
Donofrio, do you have something else to say?

DONOFRIO:
Regina, this is my family . . . They are my reason to live, they are . . . they're all I have. (He nods at all three women.) Sometimes our human nature betrays us . . . with our territorial behavior . . . our (scoffs) magnified sense of self-worth . . . selfishness. In other words, plain-old, senseless human nature!

KIRA:
Dono, please forgive me!

(The two hug. CARMEN looks over to them from her spot on the floor.)

CARMEN:
By the way, guys, those oranges are bitter. Ugh!

ALEXA:
Dono, next time you buy oranges, get the organic ones. They do have better quality and flavor.

DONOFRIO:
But Alexa, you always ask me to buy the cheapest.

ALEXA:
Well, not anymore, Dono. We should not waste time trying to save a few pennies on cheap food. Instead, we should enjoy more flavorful oranges, apples . . . berries . . . colorful landscapes, full of delicate scents and aromas . . . all of us together, as a loving family . . . a family that has forgotten love is a gift of GOD, on a daily basis . . .

(She smiles and looks at them, and once more, they all hug.)

CARMEN:
By the way, Regina, I'm sorry, but I have to ask after all this . . . What is in the bag you gave my mom to guard for you?

DONOFRIO:
Actually, Carmen, I have the bag with me. Here, Regina. If you don't trust us with it any longer, I would completely understand.

REGINA:
I did trust you with it, Dono. And I still do. That was the whole idea.

KIRA:
(Eagerly) So what was in the bag then? (Ahem) Unless you mind me asking, that is.

REGINA:
(Shrugs) Money.

FAMILY:
MONEY?!

REGINA:
Yes, money that I wanted to hide from my husband. So that no-account rascal doesn't steal it from me.

FAMILY:
But you said . . .

REGINA:
(To audience) Oh, I know what I said . . . I better leave! I just remembered a fifty-dollar bill I left in the cookie

jar. (Aside) I should've hid it under the broccoli. He'd never find it there . . .

(REGINA exits. The family looks between each other awkwardly, uncertain what to do or say next.)

DONOFRIO:
(Looking at KIRA tenderly) I know you have always meant well. Would you forgive me?

KIRA:
Dono, deep in my heart, believe it or not, you are a son to me. You know that, right?

(DONOFRIO nods affirmatively. The family warmly hugs while very soft music plays in the background, and a spotlight is directed to them only. KIRA looks at the bag of oranges, and takes out a single orange. She hesitates and then begins to peel it. She removes a section and hands it to DONOFRIO. He reaches out to take it, and the moment he touches it, all characters freeze.)

(LIGHTS OUT)

CURTAIN

The Box of Bandages

CAST:

MRS. KRONBERG
LUPE FUTZ
DODIE PARCHOOT
PETULA VATIALI
REAH CHON-MI
DODIE'S MOTHER
DODIE'S FATHER
LUPE'S MOTHER
LUPE'S FATHER

NARRATOR:

Living in the South, for many, is a curse. You see . . . throughout the history of this country, the shadow of slavery has been identified as a consequence of how things go south in the South, but not many Yankees will admit that. While they have to endure the monotonous gloom of their snowy winters, the weather is more pleasant here. It is romantic, cheerful, and enjoyable to see the scenes through the snowy windows, depicted in the movies; it really makes you want to be there, drinking a nice cup of hot chocolate . . . Oh! What a blissful image!

In the South, one can have a beautiful snow blizzard and in four hours, that snowman, which took forty-five minutes to create, will be melting when the rain starts pouring. There is a wishful thinking that arrives after the snow falls . . . The rain pours, washing away the roads to make them look just barely wet.

I am going to tell you about the day, here in our beautiful South, Dixieland, when it snowed, rained, and the roads became icy skating rinks. When the mystical, magical icicles hung from the trees everywhere; the day when our city became stuck in time, and space, all due to the beautiful snow turned ice.

At three p.m., local officials declared a state of emergency, and everybody was urged to return home as soon as possible . . .

But at Caprice School, before final dismissal, a group of older kids were left alone in the entire school. Most everyone had left by two p.m. earlier that day.

(The scene takes place during an icy, dark afternoon, in a school classroom with a big window located two feet above the floor, which can be opened as a door. The room is composed of several tables and chairs, a whiteboard, and a big teacher's desk with a chair; on top of it, there is a visible folded blanket. There is an adult counselor and four tween girls, all with big name tags.)

MRS. KRONBERG:
Girls, I'm leaving right now! I have to check on my family!

LUPE:
Mrs. Kronberg, what's happening out there? Where is everybody?

MRS. KRONBERG:
The emergency alarm rang earlier and everyone was evacuated. The streets are icy, and all the cars are slipping. I even heard about school buses stranded in the streets and highways.

DODIE:
Oh no!

(DODIE starts sucking her thumb and walks toward a window to look outside. LUPE FUTZ, another young girl, timidly holds closer her stuffed doll and starts quietly whispering to it.)

MRS. KRONBERG:
Anyway girls, I . . . I really have to leave . . . (Frantic) Don't you dare leave this room. Don't open any door or window!

PETULA:
(Stands up) What did you say your name was?

MRS. KRONBERG:
Petula! I am your school counselor . . . Don't you know
my name after all these years?

PETULA:
Ah! I see! School counselor you said? That's why I
don't know your name. Ha!

LUPE:
What is that supposed to mean?

PETULA:
(Looks intensely at LUPE's name tag and attempts to
pronounce her name) LOO-PEE . . . Huh! Forget it!
Counselors are for losers. That's probably why I
don't know who she is.

MRS. KRONBERG:
Petula . . . (Fumes briefly, then stops herself.) You can
thank the forces of nature that I am rushing to check
on my family!

PETULA:
So! What's your point? (Defiantly) You are leaving,
right? (She motions flippantly) Then go!

MRS. KRONBERG:
(To all girls) Don't go anywhere! Do you hear me?
And . . . and keep your phones charged!

LUPE:
(Frantic) Are you really leaving, Mrs. Kronberg?

MRS. KRONBERG:

I . . . I have to, dear. (Looks uncertainly back at the girls for a moment, reconsidering) I have to . . . I have to reach my family!

PETULA:

You know . . . after all this is over, my parents are going to sue you, whatever your name is! So . . . leave! (Scoffs) Get the heck out of here!

LUPE:

Take us with you, please?

MRS. KRONBERG:

I'm sorry Lupe, I can't . . . (Holding back tears)

PETULA:

So useless! I am going to nail you. You are going to lose everything. Whatever you said your name is.

MRS. KRONBERG:

I don't care how much anger you have toward me at this moment, Petula Vatiali. At this crucial time, I have to watch out for my own family. If I don't . . . no one will.

DODIE and LUPE:

Please take us with you.

MRS. KRONBERG:

(Crying at this point) I can't . . . legally I can't, my dears . . . Believe me. Goodbye. (Exits the scene still crying)

(DODIE and LUPE cry frantically. PETULA sits in a chair and looks to the window while rolling her eyes at the others. Finally fed up, she suddenly reacts and starts yelling at the other girls.)

PETULA:
Shut up! Shut up! Shut up! Ughhh . . . What a bunch of
   useless losers I have to be stuck with.

(Finally realizing their protests are futile, the rest of
the girls disperse and quiet down. LUPE checks her
phone.)

LUPE:
I don't have a signal on my phone! Oh no. Mom? Dad?
   Please? Somebody answer!

(REAH CHON-MI, who wears her hair covering half
of her face, dials a number in her cell phone and talks.)

REAH:
Hello? Where are you? Can you please reach out to my
   sister?
Hello? Hello!

(REAH looks at her phone in disbelief for a moment,
sighs.)

PETULA:
Who were you calling?

REAH:
She's a friend of mine. She's safe . . . She was picked up
   before the early car rider dismissal by her parents.
   She's at her house now.

PETULA:
What a waste of time! Why didn't you call your parents? Instead, you called a freaking friend?

REAH:
Just so that you know, I am not allowed to call them while they are at work . . . before six p.m.

PETULA:
Give me that phone! I will call them myself!

REAH:
No! Give it back! Give it back!

(PETULA fends her off, then after scanning down the phone briefly, apparently finds what she's looking for. She dials . . . waits, and then wrinkles her nose, seemingly not getting a response. She stares coldly at REAH and then mockingly reacts, as though being completely surprised.)

PETULA:
WOW! It went straight to voicemail. (Laughs)

REAH:
Give it to me! (Cries) I told you, I can't call them before six p.m., didn't I?

LUPE:
But Reah, today is a disaster day! (Points to the window) Look! There is ice everywhere. What if something happened to your parents, Reah?

REAH:
They are very busy at work! They own a franchised restaurant chain. They are very important people, you know.

PETULA:
Important people? Your parents are really important people? (Scoffs) MY parents are really important

people! They own a corporation that produces computer parts to be sold internationally!

LUPE:
I know who your parents are, Petula.

PETULA:
There! All of you are a bunch of retards . . . (Stands up) and I don't know how long we will be here, but you all will do as I say, and that is . . . to stay . . . QUIET!

(All this time, DODIE has spent gazing at a point in the room. Then she turns slowly and starts staring at PETULA.)

PETULA:
Of all the children walking in this world, I have to be here with you. The most useless of all! Not even the school counselor wants you!
(All the girls remain silent.)

LUPE:
She didn't want you either, Petula!

PETULA:
You know her and she knows you. We don't know each other. Are you losing it? Tell me . . . what serious problems do you have . . . to need the school counselor? Are you an overeater? A . . . a loner perhaps? A good-for-nothing is what you are! Ha-ha!

REAH:
Stop it! Stop it right now!

PETULA:
Ooh! Ooh! So it's you? Or maybe all of you in this sad

room need counseling. I'm leaving. I have to get out of this room right now!

LUPE:
(Fearfully) What do you mean?

PETULA:
This is not the place for me, a Vatiali! I don't belong here. Don't you see?

LUPE:
Please! Don't leave! Don't leave! Petula, we have to stay together, please!

REAH:
Why do you want her to be here? Let her go! She's a bully. She always HAS been a bully!

LUPE:
(Still fearful) But we are alone in this building and don't know what's going on out there. By the way, how come we never heard the emergency alarm buzzing? Did any of you hear it?
(All of them shake their heads, indicating they didn't. LUPE wanders closer to DODIE.)

LUPE:
Hey, say something! Did you hear anything?

DODIE:
(Staring blankly at LUPE) Who, me? Are you ... talking to me?

PETULA:
(Scoffs) This is ridiculous! (She stares down DODIE and tries to pronounce her name while looking at her name tag) DODIE PAR-CHOO–HOOT. "PARACHUTE!" Ha! Yes, you!

DODIE:

No, I didn't hear anything; I just know my parents come to pick me up at 6:30 p.m. every day, so . . . I just mind my own business.

REAH:

Dodie, are you always at the after-school period here?

DODIE:

Yes! Every day. Are you, too?

REAH:

Of course! Every day . . . after my soccer practice.

LUPE:

So, you all know Mr. Parcel?

PETULA:

Of course, I know him! Where is he, by the way?

LUPE:

Probably never left his home because of the ice. Lucky!

DODIE:

Are all of us in this room part of the after-school program?

ALL:

(Together) Yes . . .

DODIE:

And none of us know each other?

LUPE:

Except for Petula here, I don't know any of you that well.

PETULA:

Who cares?

LUPE:
What do you mean, "Who cares?" That might be the very reason we all are here stuck in this room!

DODIE:
I don't mean to change the subject, but I'm hungry!

(LUPE begins to cry.)

PETULA:
Hungry? You just have to suck your thumb like you always do! Ha ha ha!

(All the girls laugh, except DODIE, who begins to cry desperately. REAH then stops laughing and becomes very serious.)

REAH:
Stop! This is not a movie, not a play. This is real! Don't . . . don't you all get it?

PETULA:
Stop what? Stop saying that I am surrounded by— (LUPE interrupts abruptly)

LUPE:
Yes, yes, yes. Losers! You already said that.

(PETULA points her finger at LUPE threateningly.)

PETULA:
Don't you EVER raise your voice at me again! You don't even know HALF of me!

LUPE:
I'm sorry! (Walks away)

PETULA:
I wanted to leave earlier . . . I should have, and maybe
    I will!

(PETULA rummages through her backpack and then
glares at DODIE.)

PETULA:
Hey, you! Thumb-sucker! Here . . . Catch!

(PETULA throws a bag of chips to her. DODIE picks
it up, opens it, and starts eating hungrily. REAH looks
hopefully over at DODIE.)

REAH:
Hey . . . Share a few chips, huh?

DODIE:
(Frantically) No!

REAH:
Fine! No worries. Hey Petula, do you have any more
    snacks?

PETULA:
No. That was it!

LUPE:
So, we don't know how long we are going to be in this
    room? And Petula just gave away the only edible
    snack we had?

PETULA:
Apparently . . . yes! So what? You know, I'm getting
    tired of you. You're a nuisance! Go ahead and stuff
    your mouth with that ugly doll of yours! Ha-ha!

(LUPE stares at her stuffed doll, pets it, and starts crying.)

PETULA:

You all said you didn't know anyone in this room before today's disaster, right? But Lupe said she knew who I was. How many of you know who I am? (All the girls raise their hands) So, there we go! I am the only one worthy of some meaning in this room.

LUPE:

Well, that's because of your posts on social media.

PETULA:

What made you look at my posts? I didn't force you, that's for sure!

REAH:

What's your point? Petula, why are you so worried about your meaning or position in this room?

PETULA:

Worried? Me? It's obvious I'm the only one who doesn't belong here. As I stated before, look at my social media replies from today. For example . . .

(All of the girls gather around her.)

PETULA:

All of them are checking on my status and wondering how and where I am.

REAH:

What good does that do to you? They are there, and you are still here, right?

PETULA:

You . . . jealous creature!

LUPE:
Stop!

(A very sudden silence emerges and lasts an awkwardly long time. Finally, PETULA gets impatient and gives REAH a disdainful glare.)

PETULA:
Hey, you . . . Why don't you uncover your face from that hair? Come on! Let me pull it back.

(PETULA walks toward REAH and forcefully tries to pull the hair from her face.)

REAH:
No! Please . . . Stay away from me!
(They both engage in a strained game of avoidance.)

PETULA:
Let me . . . pull it . . . back!

(PETULA pulls the hair from REAH's face. REAH then steps back, looking flabbergasted at the rest of the group. All of the other girls are astonished as they notice a very long scar crossing REAH's right cheek.)

PETULA:
That's all? A scar? Oh, come on!

(REAH starts crying and the rest of the girls surround her to console her.)

DODIE:
(Emphatically) Now, that's ENOUGH!

REAH:
I am not going to allow you to keep bullying any of us anymore, Petula!

PETULA:
Aw, yeah? What are you going to do? Huh? Dodie, you thumb-sucker? Are you going to keep sucking your thumb until you grow a sprout of corn there? Ha-ha!

DODIE:
(Sobbing) Oh . . . you!

LUPE:
(To PETULA) Well, you've attacked everybody else, what are you going to say about me, huh?

PETULA:
Not much. Just "STUFFING"! Ha-ha-ha!

(PETULA walks and sits in a chair, casually checking her cell phone. In the middle of the room, the scene is dark, except for one light shining on the characters. DODIE stares at her own thumb while LUPE stares at her doll and REAH covers her face with her hands.)

REAH:
Why are we here? (Sobbing) Why are we here? So . . . So alone?

(The lights dim down slowly, until the scene becomes completely dark.)

INTERMISSION

REAH:

Why doesn't anyone care about us? (Crying) We have been here for hours, now.

PETULA:

No one cares about us. So what! Who cares? I don't care whether or not people care about me!

DODIE:

That sure explains why you are . . . well . . . the brat you are.

PETULA:

So what? Am I a brat? Yes! I'm proud of it. That, my dears, is exactly why I have so many followers. And from now on, you all are going to remain quiet and do what I TELL you to do!

DODIE:

Oh yeah? And why? Who gave you that right?

PETULA:

Because I am the only one that can say what has to be done.

DODIE:

I once heard that everyone has something important to say! And so does everyone in this room.

(The remaining girls stand up and look straight at PETULA.)

PETULA:

(Starts clapping) What a good act you three losers have come up with. Bravo! Here-here . . . and here! (She throws a hair scrunchie to REAH.) This will hold that hair off your face for GOOD this time!

REAH:
(Catches the scrunchie and holds it bewilderedly.)
What is this supposed to mean? I don't need this!
(She tosses the scrunchie on the floor.)

PETULA:
I should have left hours ago!

LUPE:
(Waves her hand grandly toward the door.) No one is
stopping you now, Petula.

PETULA:
Is that so? (She takes out her phone and dials a num-
ber) Yes? David, it's me, Petula . . . (Pauses briefly)
Because I did not WANT to answer it, that's WHY!
I don't care! (Pause) What did they say? (Pause) Ah!
Okay . . . Yes, yes, whatever! Ugh . . . I'll wait! Bye!

LUPE:
What happened? Who was that?

PETULA:
My parents have sent a helicopter to pick me up. It
should be arriving any minute.

REAH:
(Hopefully) Are you going to take us with you?

PETULA:
What do you expect, after all this? (Scoffs) Of course
not! You are out of your mind.

(Helicopter sounds approach, and all the girls look to
one another nervously.)

PETULA:
(Looking through the window) There it is! (For a brief moment she stares at the rest of the girls almost sadly then pauses briefly.) Time to go!

(PETULA approaches the window, opens it wide, and looks behind her toward the rest of the girls; all lock their glances to one another. PETULA jumps out and leaves the scene. The rest of the girls walk toward the window and stare as the helicopter takes off slowly.)

DODIE:
I can't believe it! She just left us here, just like that . . .

LUPE:
And left us, left us, left us . . . (She locks her glance at the floor.)

REAH:
We don't need her! We don't need anyone like her!

DODIE:
(Shivering, and sobbing) Ooh, I am freezing!

(The other two girls gather around her and all hug to warm up for few seconds.)

REAH:
Wait!

(REAH walks toward the teacher's desk and takes a blanket that is lying on top. She unfolds it and wraps DODIE with it.)

REAH:
Better?

DODIE:
Yes. Thank you, Reah. By the way, (She reaches inside of one of her pockets and takes out a bag of snacks.) Here, take it.

LUPE:
Didn't you eat it earlier, when Petula gave it to you?

DODIE:
Not all. I was saving it for later, but I think this is the right time.

REAH:
Thank you, I am REALLY starving . . . (She takes a few pieces out of the bag.)

DODIE:
Do you want some, Lupe?

LUPE:
Keep it, Dodie, in case we have to be here longer . . . (Starts sobbing and looks at cell phone.)

LUPE:
My parents are desperate, they don't know what to do, and they already called the police . . . They said in this text message to let them know we're trapped here . . . (Keeps sobbing)

DODIE:
(Checks her cell phone.) Mine are sad too. They haven't been able to get out of their car on the highway! My mom is crying. (She begins sobbing.)

REAH:
Dodie, are you feeling warmer now?

DODIE:

Yes . . . I am feeling much better! (She hesitates.) Say, um . . . Reah . . . how did you get that scar on your face?

LUPE:

Dodie! What on earth? Don't ask that!

REAH:

It's okay, Lupe . . . There was this car accident, and I got some injuries here and there; this is one of them.

DODIE:

Were you in the front or the back?

LUPE:

Stop it, Dodie! (Scoffs) Maybe NOW you should stick that thumb in your mouth!

REAH:

Neither Dodie. I was at home playing peacefully when a car smashed the side wall of my house. (REAH stares at the window, lost in her thoughts.)

LUPE:

(To DODIE) Are you happy now? Look what you've done!

DODIE:

Reah, I didn't mean to . . . I'm so sorry for asking about your accident.

REAH:

When you're not sucking your thumb, you ask lots of questions.

(All the girls laugh together.)

LUPE:
Reah, is that why you let your hair cover your face all the time?

DODIE:
Oh, Lupe, who's asking dumb questions now, huh?

(All the girls laugh again.)

DODIE:
Reah, I think you're prettier without that hair covering your face.

LUPE:
I agree! Where is that scrunchie Petula gave you? (She glances around.) Ah! There it is. (She picks it up.) Here! (She approaches REAH, and holds her hair in a ponytail with the scrunchie.)

DODIE:
Wow, Reah! You . . . you look so different!

REAH:
Don't do that! (Sobs)

LUPE:
Your scar looks so freaking cool! I mean, you know, you . . . You look like a rebel, girl!

DODIE:
Yeah, girl! You rock!

REAH:
(Intermittent sobbing) Really?

LUPE:

Do you know that there are people who pay for tattoos that look like real scars? (Scoffs) Well, you don't have to, Reah. I mean . . . WOW!

REAH:

(Thoughtfully) Lupe . . . What would you do . . . if I took your doll?

LUPE:

Reah, why would you do that? What have I done to you?

REAH:

Lupe, you don't need that doll . . . You know that, right?

LUPE:

I know that's none of your business. Ugh! Don't you dare touch it!

REAH:

It's okay, Lupe, I won't touch it, but . . . you should think about it. You know, that doll isn't feeding you, or warming you up from this icy weather.

DODIE:

(To LUPE) Hey, we're not like Petula Vatiali. We might observe, but we can't judge you.

LUPE:

This doll makes me feel at home. I keep him inside my backpack so that my rude classmates don't make fun of me during class. Then, in the after-school period, I keep it close to me; no one cares who I am anyway.

REAH:
I rarely see my parents. Barely know them, actually.

LUPE:
Me either, I never see them. They're always busy, and if they are at home . . . (Sighs) they're still working.

DODIE:
So, your doll makes it seem as if . . . your parents are with you?

LUPE:
No! With my doll near, I feel at home, where no one can hurt me.

REAH:
Girls! Do you hear something?

DODIE and LUPE:
No, what?

REAH:
Like a helicopter?

DODIE:
Actually, uh . . . sort of.

(The girls approach the window, and the sound of the helicopter intensifies. MRS. KRONBERG appears through the window, walks over the window sill, and stands in front of the three girls. She looks visibly relieved.)

MRS. KRONBERG:
Girls! Are you okay?

REAH:
Mrs. Kronberg! What the freak are you doing here?

DODIE and LUPE:
Yes? (Flabbergasted)

MRS. KRONBERG:
When I arrived home, once I saw all my own children
were fine, and the relief I felt . . . all at once, I could
not stop thinking about you trapped here! It was
wrong of me to leave you, I'm so sorry, I shouldn't
have. I panicked, and . . . Can you, please, ever forgive me?

(All three girls and MRS. KRONBERG hug and cry.)

LUPE:
But, how? The helicopter? Mrs. Kronberg?

MRS. KRONBERG:
Ah, yes! Petula's parents were kind enough to lend its
service for us.

DODIE:
Petula's parents? (Scoffs) That's hard to believe . . .

MRS. KRONBERG:
Actually, girls, when I called Petula's parents, she
asked THEM to use the helicopter to rescue you.

REAH:
Mrs. Kronberg, you called Petula's parents? What
about OUR parents? What's so special about them,
and . . . why not ours? (She angrily places her hands
on her hips in defiance.)

MRS. KRONBERG:
Actually, Reah, I DID call all of your parents. Hold on,
girls! (She approaches the window) Parents! Where
are you?

(All three girls' parents cross the window sill and enter the scene—very dramatic brief silence—each of the girls approach their own parents. Everybody sobs.)

REAH'S MOM:
We were so sad, desperate, and hopeless with you stranded here! I am so sorry, Reah, please, forgive us!

REAH:
Mom, I don't have anything to forgive . . . You two are here!

REAH'S FATHER:
No, Reah . . . This is not right! (Sobs) After the accident, with all the medical bills that we had to pay, we decided to work in the restaurant, and basically abandoned you!

REAH'S MOM:
Don't say that!

REAH'S FATHER:
Yes . . . It is the tragic truth. Don't contradict me! You know it is true.

REAH'S MOM:
Reah, you and your older sister are still children, that is why we have decided that I am not going to work all the time at the restaurant, just in the mornings, while the two of you are in school.

REAH:
Do you mean it, Mom?

REAH'S MOM:

Really, Reah. The pain and desperation, and the frustration your dad and I have felt during these last few hours have led us to that decision.

REAH:

Thank you. (She cries and hugs her parents.)

LUPE'S MOM:

Lupe, we've had the chance to talk with the Parchoots, and decided that you two are never going to be in the after-school program here . . . or ANY other school.

(LUPE hugs her parents and DODIE hugs hers as well.)

MRS. KRONBERG:

Well, I hate to break this very beautiful and emotional scene but we have to get to the helicopter. The weather is still dangerous out there! Besides, the pilot just texted; if we stay much longer, we would risk having ice forming in the spinners.

(PETULA crosses the window sill.)

PETULA:
Hello there!

LUPE:
PETULA!

DODIE:
I thought you left us alone. What are you doing here?

PETULA:
Saving your freaking rear ends! Don't you see?

REAH:
Petula, you never change!

MRS. KRONBERG:
Reah, Petula asked her parents to bring your parents along.

LUPE:
So, what you're saying, Mrs. Kronberg, is that we have to be . . . grateful to Petula?

DODIE:
After all the awful things she said to us while she was stuck with us here?

MRS. KRONBERG:
Maybe not grateful, but it gives you something to think about, girls. And I am going to say this in front of your parents . . . Why were these four girls the only ones that missed hearing the emergency alarm? Why are they the only ones remaining in this school of two thousand students?

DODIE'S MOM:
(Angrily) So, Mrs. Kronberg, what you're saying is that they remained here, because we're bad parents?

MRS. KRONBERG:
Oh no, Mrs. Parchoot! What I AM saying is . . . It's because they all live in their own little worlds, where nothing else matters; each had her own security bubble, and the events of the last few hours have proven that those bubbles had to burst. As the school counselor, I know three of these girls; they all have come to my office clinic in their own separate ways, and they all have come together today. Is it a coincidence? Of course not . . . At least, I don't think so.

PETULA:
Ha-ha . . . Losers!

MRS. KRONBERG:
Oh no, Petula! The difference between these three girls and you is your pride . . . That superiority complex of yours!

PETULA:
(Angrily) You scarecrow . . . My parents pay your miserable salary, and I can have them take it from you! You ungrateful—Ugh! My helicopter brought you all here, didn't it?

REAH:
Maybe you brought them all here to calm your own conscience, after all, you left us abandoned behind! Because, Petula, you also were here with us, all alone after the school was evacuated. There is not much difference between you and us.

PETULA:
Yes, with all of you losers, the thumb-sucker, the stuffed-doll holder, and this freak! Who has that creepy scar! Now, I understand why you have to cover your face! Ha-ha!

REAH:
Do you see me covering it anymore? I am holding my hair with the scrunchie YOU gave me. Look at my face, Petula! I survived the accident that left this scar! And NOW, I am finally free, free, free . . . and I have accepted it.

DODIE:
Girls! (Breathlessly) I haven't sucked my thumb in the last hour . . . Oh my!

(REAH, and LUPE nod.)

PETULA:
But you, Lupe . . . Look at you still holding your ugly
doll . . .

(PETULA approaches LUPE, abruptly takes the doll,
and throws it on the floor. LUPE runs to her parents'
arms and cries.)

DODIE'S MOM:
PETULA VATIALI! Who gave you the right to such a
careless act? At least the parents of the other girls are
here. What about your parents, Petula?

PETULA:
You . . . ungrateful—(Gasps)

MRS. KRONBERG:
Enough, Petula! Enough!

(All is silent, lights shine only on PETULA. She is shaking, and looking all around her. Tears come down her
cheeks but she does not make a sound.)

MRS. KRONBERG:
Petula, what's my name?

PETULA:
I don't know, and I simply don't need to know it.

MRS. KRONBERG:
Because, Petula, you also live in your own security
bubble, where no one else exists, where your non-
chalant parents' absence won't hurt you!

PETULA:

I am stronger than all of you combined! (She wags her index finger at all of them.) I don't need my parents like all you weak links do! I am a survivor! I don't need anyone! (She glares at the audience.)

LUPE:

Petula, but you are here!

(PETULA and LUPE exchange looks.)

PETULA:

Earlier, when the shrink called my parents, I actually DID beg them to send the helicopter to rescue you. I honestly did NOT want to care . . . (Sighs) But I did.

(All the girls run and hug PETULA. All four girls cry together for a few seconds. PETULA walks over, picks up the doll from the floor, and gives it back to LUPE.)

PETULA:

I don't understand why you like to hold this awful thing . . . but I should not even have touched it. You have to be stronger than that, Lupe.

MRS. KRONBERG:

(Looking out the window) Girls, the pilot is commanding us to go now! Go . . . Go! Go!

(MRS. KRONBERG points frantically to the window. All the parents obey, exit through the window first, while MRS. KRONBERG stands by, helping them across.)

PETULA:
Reah! Do you want to take off the scrunchie from your
    hair? You know you can keep it if you want!

REAH:
No, Petula, I want to keep it, if that it's okay with you.

PETULA:
Whatever!

(Both REAH and PETULA exit the window.)

LUPE:
(To DODIE, pointing to her doll) Should I bring it?

DODIE:
(Shrugs) It's your call, Lupe.

LUPE:
(After a thoughtful pause) Nah!

(LUPE walks toward the desk and very carefully places
the doll at the center. She stares at it for few seconds.)

DODIE:
Here!

(DODIE takes a box of bandages out of her backpack
and puts the box next to the doll.)

LUPE:
What are those, Dodie?

DODIE:
The bandages I used to cover my thumb's callous . . .
    (Shows the knuckle of her thumb to DODIE.) I won't
    need them anymore.

LUPE:
Sure?

DODIE:
(Looks intensely to her own thumbs) Sure! Actually, VERY sure, Lupe.

MRS. KRONBERG:
Girls! Come . . . Come!

LUPE:
Now, come on, Dodie, Let's go!

DODIE:
Yes Lupe! Let's!

(DODIE and LUPE exit the window while laughing. MRS. KRONBERG slowly glances around the entire room and sees the doll on the desk, walks toward it, and grabs it. She walks toward the window, stops, and glances down at the doll. After a thoughtful pause, she goes back and walks to the desk again. She very carefully places the doll back, then walks to the window, and exits. The scene turns dark and the spotlight shines only on the doll, while music is playing softly for few seconds.)

(Lights out.)

THE END

About the Author

Albalis Vargas-Smith, a.k.a. Lirio Blanco Show, is an architect, painter, muralist, and writer from Panama. She received her undergraduate and graduate degrees in architecture from Universidad Autonoma de Centroamerica in San Jose, Costa Rica. In addition, she received a bachelor degree in fine arts at Auburn University, Montgomery. She has more than twenty years of experience in architecture, having worked both in Montgomery, Alabama, and the Atlanta area. She has done theatrical scene and set design as volunteer work for community theatre groups.

Back in July 2016, Albalis went solo as an entrepreneur architect, founding the Vargas-Smith Studio. The reason? To spend more time with her daughter. In 2020, she decided to finish a series of backburner short stories and theatrical plays, which are presented in this book.

Currently, Albalis lives in Johns Creek, Georgia, with her daughter, husband, her dog, Toni, and two precious birds.

To Milana   From Steph

www.ingramcontent.com/pod-product-compliance
Lightning Source LLC
Chambersburg PA
CBHW050458110726
47899CB00003B/989